KT-447-858

60000410560

Northamptonshire Libraries & Information Service CC	
Askews & Holts	

Funny Footprints

by **Katie Dale** and **Nanette Regan**

W
FRANKLIN WATTS
LONDON•SYDNEY

Ben woke up and smiled.

It was his birthday

and it was snowing.

Hurray!

"Let's go for a walk," said Dad.

Dad and Ben went to the park.

"Look at all our footprints!"

Ben laughed.

Then Ben saw something in the snow.

He stopped.

"Look, Dad. How odd!" he said.

"Funny footprints."

"The footprints look like zigzags,"
said Ben.

"What made them?"

"Let's follow them and find out,"
said Dad.

Who made the footprints in the snow?
Let's follow them to see where they go.

They followed the footprints into the wood.

Dad sang a little song.

"Look, Dad," said Ben.

"More funny footprints!

They look like long lines."

Who made the footprints
in the snow?
Let's follow them
to see where they go.

Dad and Ben followed the footprints

over the bridge.

"Dad! Look over here!" shouted Ben.
"There are some
more funny footprints!
What made them?"

Who made the footprints
in the snow?
Let's follow them
to see where they go.

Dad and Ben followed the footprints

along the river.

"Dad, now there are
some footprints like spots, too!"

There were zigzags,

two long lines,

holes and a footprint,

and some spots.

12

Who made the footprints
in the snow?
Let's follow them
to see where they go.

13

The footprints went down the road ...

and into Ben's garden.

How odd!

Ben looked at Dad.

"Open the gate," said Dad.

"Let's see what made

all those funny footprints."

Ben opened the gate, very slowly.

He saw ...

Dan on his rollerblades,

Meg in her wheelchair,

Granddad with his bad leg,

and Tim on his pogo stick.

"Happy birthday, Ben!"

everyone cried.

"Did our footprints

spoil the surprise?" asked Granddad.

"No!" laughed Ben.

"They made it even better!"

Story order

Look at these 5 pictures and captions.
Put the pictures in the right order
to retell the story.

1

Ben and Dad walked over the bridge.

2

Ben looked out of the window.

3

Ben got a birthday cake.

4

Ben and Dad went into the park.

5

Ben opened the gate.

21

Independent Reading

This series is designed to provide an opportunity for your child to read on their own. These notes are written for you to help your child choose a book and to read it independently.

In school, your child's teacher will often be using reading books which have been banded to support the process of learning to read. Use the book band colour your child is reading in school to help you make a good choice. *Funny Footprints* is a good choice for children reading at Orange Band in their classroom to read independently.

The aim of independent reading is to read this book with ease, so that your child enjoys the story and relates it to their own experiences.

About the book

It's Ben's birthday and it's snowing. He goes for a walk with Dad. They discover some funny footprints in the snow and decide to follow them. The footprints lead them back home, and Ben discovers a birthday surprise waiting for him.

Before reading

Help your child to learn how to make good choices by asking: "Why did you choose this book? Why do you think you will enjoy it?" Look at the cover together and ask: "What do you think the story will be about?" Ask your child to think of what they already know about the story context. Then ask your child to read the title aloud. Ask: "Where do you think they see the funny footprints? Where is the story set?" Remind your child that they can sound out the letters to make a word if they get stuck.

Decide together whether your child will read the story independently or read it aloud to you.

During reading

Remind your child of what they know and what they can do independently. If reading aloud, support your child if they hesitate or ask for help by telling the word. If reading to themselves, remind your child that they can come and ask for your help if stuck.

After reading

Support comprehension by asking your child to tell you about the story. Use the story order puzzle to encourage your child to retell the story in the right sequence, in their own words. The correct sequence can be found on the next page.

Help your child think about the messages in the book that go beyond the story and ask: "Do you think Dad knew what had made the funny footprints? Why/why not?"

Give your child a chance to respond to the story: "Did you have a favourite part? Did you guess what had made any of the footprints while you were reading?"

Extending learning

Help your child understand the story structure by using the same sentence patterning and adding different elements. "Let's make up a new story about funny footprints. What can you think of that would make a funny footprint? Think about where you might like your story to happen – the footprints could be in sand on a beach or in mud in the woods, for example. Where will your footprints be?"

In the classroom, your child's teacher may be teaching the use of commas to separate items in a list. There are examples in this book that you could look at with your child. Look together at the lists on pages 12 and 16.

Franklin Watts
First published in Great Britain in 2017
by The Watts Publishing Group

Copyright © The Watts Publishing Group 2017

All rights reserved.

Series Editors: Jackie Hamley and Melanie Palmer
Series Advisors: Dr Sue Bodman and Glen Franklin
Series Designer: Peter Scoulding

A CIP catalogue record for this book is
available from the British Library.

ISBN 978 1 4451 5427 5 (hbk)
ISBN 978 1 4451 5428 2 (pbk)
ISBN 978 1 4451 6103 7 (library ebook)

Printed in China

Franklin Watts
An imprint of
Hachette Children's Group
Part of The Watts Publishing Group
Carmelite House
50 Victoria Embankment
London EC4Y 0DZ

An Hachette UK Company
www.hachette.co.uk

www.franklinwatts.co.uk

FSC
www.fsc.org
MIX
Paper from
responsible sources
FSC® C104740

Answer to Story order: 2, 4, 1, 5, 3